BLOOD GUILT

Also by Robert Franklin Gish from Sunstone Press:

Twilight Troubadour

Blood Guilt

A Story of Atonement

First in the Salinas Trilogy

Robert Franklin Gish

SUNSTONE PRESS

SANTA FE

Blood Guilt is a work of fiction and not intended to portray or dramatize any dead or living individual. It is solely the product of the author's imagination, intended to entertain rather than instruct. Fiction, however, often has its own brand of truth.

—RFG

Sunstone books may be purchased for educational, business, or sales promotional use.
For information please write: Special Markets Department, Sunstone Press,
P.O. Box 2321, Santa Fe, New Mexico 87504-2321.

Design › R. Ahl
Printed on acid-free paper
eBook 978-1-61139-640-9

Library of Congress Cataloging-in-Publication Data

Names: Gish, Robert, author. | Gish, Robert Salinas trilogy ; 1st.
Title: Blood guilt : a story of atonement / by Robert Franklin Gish.
Description: Santa Fe, NM : Sunstone Press, [2021] | Series: Salinas
   trilogy ; 1st | Summary: "This novella of becoming traces the growth of
   a young bi-racial woman's struggles in life and love, marriage and
   motherhood as she leaves the home she must leave only to be drawn back
   by the forces of destiny"-- Provided by publisher.
Identifiers: LCCN 2021039704 | ISBN 9781632933614 (paperback) | ISBN
   9781611396409 (epub)
Subjects: LCSH: Racially mixed women--New Mexico--Fiction. | Hispanic
   Americans--Fiction.
Classification: LCC PS3557.I79 B55 2021 | DDC 813/.54--dc23
LC record available at https://lccn.loc.gov/2021039704

WWW.SUNSTONEPRESS.COM
SUNSTONE PRESS / POST OFFICE BOX 2321 / SANTA FE, NM 87504-2321 /USA
(505) 988-4418

For AK with affection

"This ain't a song for the broken hearted.
No silent prayer for faith departed.
I ain't gonna be no face in the crowd.
You're gonna hear my voice when
I shout it out loud.
It's my life.
It's now or never.
Cause I ain't gonna live forever.
I just want to live while I'm alive."
—Bon Jovi

"These signs will accompany those who have believed:
In My name they will cast out demons; they will speak
with new tongues; they will pick up serpents; and if
they drink any deadly poison, it will not hurt them;
they will lay hands on the sick, and they will recover."
—Mark 16:15-18

"Of remedies of love she knew *per chaunce*
For she koude of tht art the olde daunce."
—Chaucer, Prologue: *The Canterbury Tales*

Contents

Acknowledgments

The following individuals assisted me greatly in the writing of this story and I thank them for their expertise and consideration: Patricia Holman; David T. Le; Darlene Vigil; Eve Hui; Rodolfo Serrano; and Judith Kay Gish, beautiful wife and stalwart companion; abiding thanks also to an "Hombre de la Luz" for sharing his enlightened, sustaining dreams; and to my dog Bix who, always close by, comforts me.

PREFACE

The landscape against which this story is set is old and enduring and holds many such stories of success and failure, blood atonement and revenge. This is but one of them as an old television series reminded us. It happens to take place in the American Southwest, southern New Mexico to be exact, in and around the town of Mountainair and the Salinas Pueblo Native American and Spanish ruins of Gran Quivira, Abo, and Quarai.

Multitudes, over generations, have crossed this land, exploring it, settling it, and leaving it. It is a varied, barren, yet ironically regenerative and prolific land known to three cultures of Native Americans, Spanish, and Anglos; a land so vast that in places it stretches out beyond measurable distance to the rim of the visible world; a land touching sky, sky touching land, a palette of colors stippled by riverside cottonwood *bosques,* foothill *chamisa,* sage, juniper, cactus, piñón—and in its heights red-barked pine, and even higher, smooth, white, stalwart stands of aspen with their love carvings and shimmering fall golden leaves.

No jungles or tropical flora, except in the minds of misplaced souls; however, all other climatic zones converge to make what the Spanish named *Nueva Granada*, and in their explorations east the *"Llano Estacado"* (because of the banners they planted to map their way). A land with enough historical and geological variety, surprise and adventure for promoters to name it the "Land of Enchantment."

Ancient peoples lived here, keepers of sheep, farmers of corn, sojourners and settlers, populating the upper river from the sublime Rio Grande valley, with pueblos and farms, rancheros and haciendas where an abundance of corn, chile, and alfalfa, apples, apricots, and pecans serve to define and circumscribe the picturesque variety of mud villages and alfalfa fields—making for a life of comparable calm: hills, and arroyos as the lower river slows down and mellows from the harrowing upper river gorge (a waterway leaving black lava rock carved deep into the earth around Taos, but expanding to a widening rendezvous with cactus and sagebrush near Brownsville, Texas.)

That gorge and its burgeoning beds and banks caused the Spanish to divide the river into *Rio Arriba* and *Rio Abajo*, said names eventually contributing to a bifurcation of cultures according to the head and mouth of the great river.

Wildlife too adapted to the ways and means of the span of the respective head and mouth of the river and the adjacent plains, hills and mountains: deer, elk, bear and lion, along with grouse, partridge, and squirrel in the mountains; antelope, quail, dove, turkey, grouse, coyotes, Gila monsters, and rattlesnakes in the hills; the river continuing on with various waterfowl—cranes and geese and herons and ducks. All accompanied by a strange population of rodents, along with prehistoric looking roadrunners, and bloody-eyed horned toads, the entourage escorted by insects—armies of butterflies, ants, beetles, grasshoppers, and cicadas.

Just who or what came first and sooner or later departed is only presumably, only partially known by scientists and myth makers, all narratives being assigned their providential geological and biological causality.

Various ruins and archeological sites still remain to offer a partial explanation of this continuing historical panorama.

Our story, however, focuses on the Salinas Native American and Spanish mission ruins of *Abo, Gran Quivera,* and *Quarai* in south central New Mexico, near the town of Mountainair, so named for the clean mountain air of the Manzano mountains sprawling high and wide to the east at the lower end of the imposing Sangre de Cristo range. Story has it that the *Manzano* or "Apple" mountains were so named because early Spanish priests planted apple orchards at their base—echoes of the Garden of Eden one supposes.

And so here, now fashioned as artifice, as fiction, an imagined portion of the amazing, culturally laminated saga continues.

El Rancho

Nina Lucero dreaded what was to happen yet she was excited too. She'd known that feeling before in the same sense that "no" is taken to mean "yes." Really more agitated and apprehensive than excited, she awakened early from a sleepless night filled with echoes of animals bleating, surreal dreams of blood, and memories, neither one of which was that easy to distinguish, both merging into their own confused and anxious half-conscious confluence.

She heard her mother in the bathroom and her father stirring in the kitchen assembling and rattling the old percolator coffee maker, and opening the can of Folgers Columbia, which he was dedicated to. Her brother Rosendo's bedroom was next to hers and he was already strumming his beloved *Paracho* guitar, he'd gotten in *Michoacan*, Mexico, and singing an old ranchero the way he started each day—spring, summer, fall or winter. The whole extended family would soon be driving up to the house, brakes screeching, motors revving, mufflers coughing, horns honking, men hollering, announcing their arrival—ready to help with the offering of the festive slaughter. Even neighbors, old and new, were invited to the celebration.

She'd seen it all before and hated it, never really comprehending the quick demarcation of sacrifice, life one minute, death the next, ever psychologically resisting people's need to kill their own livestock which they fed and tended only to obliterate the movement and the sound and the sweet stink of their blood and lives. The Bible justified human rule over animals. God had made the beasts and the fishes for man's use. She could quote scripture of that, thanks to her mother and her father's church faith and its various assemblies of principles and beliefs.

The girl, however, was reluctant to believe all the stories drilled into her mind, heard Sunday after Sunday, especially when it came to her beloved pet sheep or her prize goats.

Insofar as she believed she made no distinction, gave no priority to the values of life between cattle, hogs, goats, and sheep—well, sheep were a little different, especially today when it was the time for a chosen lamb to die. After all, Christ was called the Lamb of God. Christ was the great shepherd who would go to any lengths to save a lost sheep or soul. Abel and his sheep were well regarded by God. So how could people, believers, not similarly sacrifice a lamb? The picture of Christ holding a forlorn lamb in his arms on a rocky hillside was etched into her mind. His flowing robes, his elegant hair, his superhuman good looks and strength. Even lambs' bleating in her dreams or outside her window seemed to ask the same question.

Any sacrifice of her goat, *Guillermo, El Chingón*, raised for the State Fair, would be hard to take and she cried just contemplating it. When anyone unthinkingly complimented her mother on her great posole and carne adovada, after Nina's personally raised hog, Lupe, found its way into winter chile, warming bellies and souls, she could hardly swallow a reply. Lupe's sacrifice would help get them through the fall and the ice storms and blizzards of winter on the llano.

The bleating of the lambs, however, coming closer outside bothered her and she turned over and curled herself up in the quilts even after Linda, her mother, yelled, "Nina, *lavantate*, it's time to rise and shine and help get ready for *la familia y la gente*. They'll be here before you know it. *Sabes qué?*"

"I know. I know...." But as she said it she was back in a partial dream to the time the whole family got up early and drove over to Chilili to hunt deer and gather piñóns. She got to ride with her uncle and aunt in their new green Chevy Silverado. The moon was still casting shadows on the ruins as they drove by Quarai. And her uncle started talking about the Lucero family heritage and how at one time they corralled and kept sheep in those very ruins—much before the state had begun their restoration. Her mother too had talked about that as part of marrying into the family and taking a job as a guide and bookstore manager at Quivera, the largest of the three ancient structures.

§

In her reverie turned dream, the eerie cloud-enshrouded November moon still shone on the stones and standing walls as they drove by Quarai.

"All the Indian spirits should be dancing over there. It's a harvest moon, some say a hunters' moon which is fitting for us. We'll beat the others there and maybe get first shot before your dad and Rosendo can load. That little flea flicker 257 Roberts your dad uses would have a hard time taking out a jack rabbit anyway; and all Rosendo cares about is his guitar and serenading his girlfriend."

She thought about the native dances and festivals she'd seen there through young excited eyes and with pounding heart, events beautifully yet curiously obvious in their being but also explained more academically by her mother, first a docent then a guide and ranger at the site.

Other than some stray cattle that had broken though their barbed wire fencing, causing her uncle, Raul, to swerve around them a time or two, Highway 55 was pretty much deserted of vehicles except for a pickup or two full of jack-lighting hunters out for a cowardly shot on opening day.

Nina was lulled by the purr of the new truck's motor and new upholstery smell and was soon off in her own world of school and friends and her infatuation with twin brothers new to Montezuma middle school. The kids had already nicknamed them Gene and Roy because of their outlandishly loud Western shirts and oversized silver rodeo belt buckles—and their bragging about how their dad had won the bronc riding competition at the Calgary Stampede and was headed for Canada's Rodeo Hall of Fame. But she thought the twin brothers, Aubrey and Lincoln, were "hot" and she fantasized about which one would be the first to ask her for a date or to a school party, or a late-night kiss if she flirted just right.

She worried a bit that her uncle was speeding but

she knew he was serious about getting to the special side road and the hunt. And sure enough, about the time she was thinking of dressing for that first imagined dance with, she guessed it would be Aubrey, her uncle pulled up short, set the emergency brake, and in no time at all had his Marlin carbine off its rear window rack and was motioning for her and her aunt Estelle to get out and head for the stand he had in mind, having scouted it out and prepared it much in advance.

Her aunt declined, saying she would wait in the truck for the others but encouraged Nina to go. "Raul is a good hunter and a safe one and will take care of you, Nina, so go. We'll all be up that way soon."

They were off fast, softly closing the truck doors, quietly climbing down and out of an arroyo, dodging rocks and cactus spines, weaving though sundry juniper trees, leaving Nina amazed at how big her uncle's stride was, trying to match the rhythm of his scuffed Wolverine boots. She'd always admired her uncle's athletic build and record as a state champion wrestler when he was in junior college down in Hobbs. He'd even shown her some basic holds like a chin lock, a bear hug, a half Nelson and a summer sault throw. He knew some Brazilian jujitsu as well and had a brown belt. "Want to see how you milk a mouse?" he would ask, then bend her little finger back on itself until she hollered "Uncle!" He was serious but funny. He was handsome as well with his long black hair, now beginning to gray around his temples, his aquiline nose, and broad chest with bulging pectorals so prominent in his summer T shirts.

When she won in arm wrestling him she knew he'd let her win. Curious in the chill morning air that summer reveries were cropping up. Raul's whispering interrupted her thoughts. "Hope Auntie uses the truck heater," she mused.

Raul interrupted her thoughts, saying softly, "We need to make it to the stand while there's still moonlight, Nina. The deer will be up and grazing for a little breakfast and I need the moonlight for a good shot."

Minutes later Nina heard something in the near distance and whispered, "*Tio*, I heard something," and before she could say more she saw it—a beautiful deer, its big ears standing alert, its mouth moving in a rhythm reminding her of her own heart beats.

"Down Nina, down *Chica*," her uncle said, seeing the deer too. "It's a doe, damn it, but fresh meat and a close shot." And before she could reply she heard the shot, a blast so loud it broke the still moonlight of the early morning, and she reached up to cover her ears, lowering her hands to see the deer bounding away.

"I hit her I'm sure!" her uncle said, standing up

to go look. Sure enough when they reached the spot where they had last seen her, they found droplets of blood, and trailing off to a little ravine they saw her body. She had been hit just a little too far behind her left leg, partially in the gut, partially in the shoulder.

"So small," Nina thought between holding back silent gasps of tears, "The hole is so, so small—and she's so young."

Then Raul slowly laid his gun down, took out his knife, seemingly in pixelated frames of movement, and slit the doe's belly open, pulling out her innards as if emptying a bowl of spaghetti or a long string of butcher shop sausages. Her stomach lurched, and . . . then . . . and then . . . an embryo, a well-formed baby deer!

"*Chingada*! Pregnant!" growled her uncle. Legal but pregnant. "*Mal suerte*, Nina! *Qué lastima*! *Pero tenemos carne.*"

§

And Nina was back in her bed crying again, sobbing, the sound of the sheep outside driving her head deep into her pillow, and she was pulling the blanket over her head, thinking so sadly again of the entrails and the embryo and how most of it, the dead little faun, and its mother's guts were just left there, fresh and steaming, waiting for the ravens and coyotes. She cried then too as Raul threw the carcass over his shoulders as easily as a sack of feathers and headed back to the truck.

"I hope he doesn't come and help dad with the sheep today," she sobbed. "Not that awful sight again. Not again!"

She rolled out of bed to the combined sounds of a .22 shot and the *rasgueos* of Rosendo's guitar. She shimmied into her jeans and pulled a turtleneck sweater over her head, enjoying the feel of the wool sliding across her budding breasts, and the restriction of its neck band, and headed out to the kitchen, stopping only for a couple of gulps of orange juice and to pick up a banana.

"You're gonna starve, *mija*," her mother warned. "And get a jacket. It's forty degrees out there."

All the activity was around the big cottonwood tree where her father and, yes, *Tio* Raul were stringing up a lamb by its hind feet, its bleating squelched, having already been killed and bled out—the vermillion blood in vast pools beneath it.

She threw her banana to the ground and gagged

as she neared the tree and the spectacle before her. The leaves were golden with fall colors, falling so wistfully and settling like a quilted blanket on the bloody tarp and ground.

"Here comes *la reina* now," her father said. Come help. Your brother's too busy playing a medley of *Malagueña* and the *Pasadobles*, pretending he's down in *Mejico* at a bullfight."

Steam was rising from the sheep's guts spilled out on the soaked-through tarp beneath it, along with the lamb's wooly-coated skin, skillfully removed as if a mere apple peel. She caught her uncle's smile— his butchering knife in hand, just like that moonlit morning when he shot the mother doe.

"It's okay, Dad. I just don't want to watch. You and *Tio* got this. I'm heading on to the barn to check on the goats. I can hear them too. They're worried they'll be next."

They didn't see her tears or hear her choked coughs as she trod on to the barn. And she didn't see the twin Crawford brothers, Aubrey and Lincoln, follow her as she wiped her eyes and sobbed her way into the barn.

"Wait for us girl," Aubrey yelled, "What are you crying about? It's just a dumb sheep."

She stopped short when she heard that and tried to arrange her hair and clear her eyes. It was them, neighborly invites, the two hottest boys in school. They were here, beside her now.

"I'm checking on my prize goat, "*Guillermo*," come and look." So they followed her to the back of the barn and the goat's pen. It was a big *Macho Cabrio* Spanish buck with long spiked horns and a shaggy face that would scare any mother's son.

What's its name, again? He's a big bastard!" Aubrey said.

"I almost named him *Pancho Villa* after the notorious bandit, or *Señor Gruff,* like in the kid's story," she said, turning in hidden apprehension to look at both of them. But no sooner than she had named the goat, saying that he was a good meat breed, than Aubrey's brother, Lincoln, grabbed her around the waist and pulled her to the ground, holding her as Aubrey had his way with her, pulling up her sweater and squeezing her breasts while his brother also rammed himself into her, still trying to hold his hand over her mouth; but she wasn't just screaming; she was applying one of the holds her uncle taught her, and moaning in pain—with reluctant, confusing pleasure too which she also tried to fight off. Lincoln was surprised at how strong she was, slipping eventually out of his grasp.

As she struggled to free herself, she wished her uncle had taught her some kind of death blow but she could only picture her goat's giant, lippy face and chewing jaws—each of the brothers' thrusts in rhythm to the goat's moving mouth. Then she envisioned again the little embryo faun wrested out of its mother, as blood ran out between Nina's legs and she saw in a tear-glazed glance the lamb strung on the big cottonwood tree outside and, thinking of Christ nailed on the cross and her shame, her blame and guilt that she had somehow asked for this. Then she fainted and lost consciousness.

How could she ever face them at school and live with not saying anything? Could she tell her mother, her father, her uncle? One thing she knew. The damn smacking noises of her goat had somehow to stop. Even the distant muffled strumming of Rosendo's guitar seemed to cry and whine and made her want to vomit.

La Escuela

The cheerleader tryouts were scheduled in the gym for Friday afternoon just after dismissal for the day. Nina had been looking forward to it for weeks, and had diligently been practicing her jumps and pompom swishes. Although she had been a "B" team cheerleader last year and knew the other cheerleader candidates well, she practiced alone. She had her rivals and her enemies but had succeeded to stand strong, thanks to her uncle's self-defense demonstrations.

There had been more than one argument and even a recent fight over position and cheer choices and hard feelings still prevailed now into the fall with football teams and drill squad choices and various club membership enlistments heating up. So Nina practiced alone under the big cottonwood in her yard at the ranch.

One girl in particular was a thorn in the

side. Jenny Duran rivaled Nina in skill but not in personality and intelligence. She was pretty enough and peppy enough but had a mean streak in her, at times deliberately tripping or pushing other girls to make them stumble or even fall. She'd caused a ruckus at the game with Magdalena. So Nina had confronted her telling her off with no uncertain words, the most explosive one being *Puta vieja.*

Nina resorted to slaps and fistfuls of hair and face scratches in addition to body and groin kicks, with no clear winner when the P.E. teacher, Miss. Fergusson, ran up and stopped them, sending them both to neutral corners on the bus ride home. Those hostilities festered through the entire school year, burgeoning into a gang fight in the spring just before the end of the term.

Jenny was there now in the fall, ready to show up her arch rival and hated antagonist, Nina. But so were all the members of last year's "B" team, including her friend, Yvonne, plus some of the girls trying out for drill squad.

Nina was popular, pretty, and smart having been named to the honor society and assistant editor of the school year book, topped off by Home Coming Queen. She was also blonde and part Anglo, the child of a Hispanic father and an Anglo mother. Much sought after by the boys, and admired by most of the girls she had her enemies too, squaring off along different ethnic lines. The one big strike against her was that the school enrollment was largely Hispanic, and she straddled two cultures as a result. Knowing Spanish and English she was viewed, ironically, as "gifted."

Nina had been especially flirtatious for over a month campaigning for the masculine vote when it came time to choose who would make and lead the "A" cheerleading squad.

She liked boys and was liked by them, given her athletic well-proportioned body and her especially alluring blue-green eyes, straight, even teeth and full lips. She knew what she was doing and ever since the Crawford bothers had forced sex upon her she admitted her ambivalence to the painfully-pleasant, violently-passionate way it was introduced. There had been more loving, more willing and consensual romances with other boys, bordering, some judged, on promiscuity. Her mother, Linda, had told her to be careful and to pick dates "fit to mate," but that distinction was a hard one to call.

She had been going steady with Rudy Abeyta, a clean-cut football player and student council president who knew the techniques of kissing. And although the Crawford brothers had leveled some innuendos, and said some incriminating things, Rudy always defended Nina's morals, seeing her flirtations as just part of loving life, and her smiles an endorsement of all humanity.

The tryouts were rigorous and she shined in her performance. So she was a shoe-in for the all-school ballot and the assembly where the vote would be taken. Jenny made the ballot too, choosing not to say a cantankerous word during the preliminaries but planning to sabotage the assembly performances.

Miss Fergusson, the P.E. teacher, asked Rudy to introduce all the candidates on assembly day. The band was playing the school song, the drill squad aspirants were there replete with dozens of pompoms. The principal, Mr. Aristides Ortega, and all of the teachers were there when Rudy took to the microphone for the introductions, all arranged alphabetically. Each candidate would get to say why they wanted to be a cheerleader, what their school involvement was, and then perform a choreographed cheer as prescribed and charted out by Miss Fergusson.

Nina came after Louise and Jenny in the presentation order, followed by two other girls, also previously on the "B" squad.

Rudy just said, "And now classmates, here's Louise Cahill. Her speech, given with a "Little Texas" drawl, was confidently exuberant but rather overblown, if not a bit embarrassing with her Jane Mansfield bosom bobbing up and down, saying she thought she was born for this role and ready to fulfill her destiny jumping to the sky and flapping her arms like a butterfly and devotedly cheering on the Monarchs.

She said she had really enjoyed being a "B" team member and gave a toothsome smile and after blowing a kiss to Nina, adding a provocative shimmy. Louise's approach to the cheer was lively and loud and she jumped and waved and kicked high and hard. If it wasn't flawless it was more than notable.

> "We're for the Monarchs
> Couldn't be prouder
> Say it soft
> Say it louder.
> Go, go Monarchs
> Show em who's boss
> Go, go Monarchs
> Put em down for a loss."

Miss Fergusson was the composer of the cheer and Louise had no objections, thinking at least it wasn't as mean spirited or nasty as some. She ended with a whisk of her short skirt, saying,

"Remember, 'Every little breeze seems to whisper L O U I S E!'"

Rudy next introduced Jenny Duran as everyone's favorite and flirty-flirty friend to all, adding "She can give em hell guys as we know." He was unashamedly stoked.

She was dressed in skin-tight short shorts and a tight-fitting T shirt with vivid, campy Mick Jagger lips on it, that complemented her fulsome figure and before saying anything, immediately did her cheer, jumping high and ending with revealing splits which caused the assembly to roar in one load groan.

Then she walked back to the microphone, saying in a sultry Katie Jurado voice, "I can't say the silly scripted cheer. This is the kind of cheer I'd give:"

Miss Ferguson was aghast when she heard Jenny's husky whisper of the following:

"Potato chips, potato chips
Crunch, crunch, crunch
Hey, all you losers
Here's your lunch!"

And she threw a finger, pointing it directly at the bleachers and then a second one at Nina, pumping her hand again and again. The assembly half roared and half groaned, then grew still when registering the blatant insult to Nina.

When it came to Nina's turn Rudy made an untoward comment when saying, "Here's the sweetheart I'm voting for, Nina Lucero! A few boos emanated from the crowd as Nina walked up to say,

"Thank you, I guess, Mr. Abeyta. And a special thank you, my "B" team gals and *Gracias a todos por tu voto.*"

Then she slowly repeated the scripted cheer, shimmied her shoulders, saluted, and threw a kiss to the stands. When she walked back to her place, with an extra wiggle in her walk she looked back over her shoulder to pat her butt and smile.

And Rudy being Rudy added to the bias of his endorsement by saying, "*Odio verete irte pero me encante verde* ; yes, I love to see "how" you leave," *Señorita Nina.*"

A couple of less popular girls without any chance of winning performed their rather sad "Fee-fi-fo-fum" cheers and then Rudy closed the assembly, trying the best he could to get out of the way of Miss Fergusson as she steamed her way over to Jenny to tell her on the spot that given the rebellious nature of her cheer she was disqualified.

Then the explosion! Jenny rushed up and pushed the shocked Miss Fergusson out of the way, then ran straight to Nina who was rising to go and walloped her with a blow straight to her face. The blood rushed from Nina's nose and she reflexively lashed out to protect herself with a swooping haymaker landing on Jenny's ear then shoulder. Then Nina, *Tio* Raul's instructions coming to mind, grabbed Jenny's hair and pulled her head down to meet Nina's knee. She then kicked her in the groin, twirling her around to get her in a chokehold. And as Jenny gasped for air, Nina threw her rival down on the floor of the stage and stomped her repeatedly from head to toe until blood flowed.

Finishing her off with a drop kick to the small of her back, leaving her bruised, bloody, and writhing in pain. All before Rudy, Mr. Ortega and a few others, including even the scurrilous Crawford twins, pulled Nina off and tried holding her, still bleeding profusely from her nose.

Aubrey turned to Lincoln, saying with obvious relief, "Damn, brother, we were lucky, looks like we riled her up!"

As the votes finally came in Jenny got the word in the hospital that Nina had won by a decided margin and been announced head cheerleader. Louise had also been elected with Yvonne, and two others drafted from the ranks of the ordinary.

Jenny cursed and vowed to her crudely tattooed friend, Martha Jimenez, who had the unlucky job of messenger, that she would kill that stuck-up, mixed-blood bitch Nina before she was through.

The feud had apparently only just begun. But Nina discovered that, all in all, she really liked fighting, enjoyed beating the crap out of Jenny, and promised to take some more training from Raul, get some fight videos, maybe join a gym and start working out. "Watch my smoke, just watch it!" she said and had the angry inspiration to cheer to herself the determination: "One and a two/Here's what I'm gonna do/Get tough. Get rough/Fight come day/Fight come night!"

But what would her folks say? Her Dad? *Tio* Raul? Rosendo and his singing guitar? Her lovely peace-loving mother Linda? And what about church? What would the new pastor say, not to mention Jesus Christ, Father, Son, and Holy Ghost, when they found out that such angry resolve resided in such a pretty, such a once innocent girl?

"Shit," Nina said. "I'm in for it now!"

La Iglesia Pentecostal

Faustine Medina was new to the small mission church. He'd seen the call when youth director at a Pentecostal church up north in Farmington.

It just so happened that he was then in a bit of hot water, accused of inappropriately touching young girls in the congregation who were usually notorious for such accusations, including one which almost ousted the preacher, Benny Benavidez, himself. It was Benny who put the idea in Faustine's head that he could easily present himself as a *bona fide* preacher blessed by Benny, the church, and God in heaven.

Benny demonstrated in service after service just how to heal certain ailments by touch or breath. He even demonstrated now and then how to praise the Lord with handling snakes! Benny had unfortunately lost his index finger when stricken by Satan's fangs in services past.

So Faustine had been eagerly looking for another

church opportunity, perhaps a revival, to preach the Gospel and heal the sick and depraved. He was a devotee of the televangelist Oral Roberts, and never missed one of his telecasts, even traveling to Tulsa to see his champion evangelist. He'd also recently been introduced to a Reverend T.D. Jakes, an up and coming Pentecostal Evangelist from Virginia by way of Texas.

Faustine practiced walking from left to right and right to left and, kneeling and sanding, in effect, strutting his stuff. Expect a miracle! Expect a miracle!" he would repeat, Bible in hand, and sternly pointing at the congregation. "*Viene un milagro!*" became his appropriated affirmation. He started overdressing and layering clothing, shirts and vests especially, in the attempt to perspire like his stereotyped charismatic Pentecostal preacher, and practiced wiping his brow with flamboyant swooshes of a colorful handkerchief.

If he ate enough bread and carbs he could gain glorious weight like the esteemed blessed, wealthy ideal.

He convinced himself that he had the gift of glossolalia as well as Xenoglossy. He prayed and he tuned in Professor Irwin Corey and Norm Crosby and practiced speaking double speak, gibberish and solecisms. He learned a few Greek, Latin, Hebrew, and even German words which he never admitted to seeing. He wasn't exactly truthful with himself, let alone with other "believers."

Since the Bible, however, justified some such things as happening on the Pentecost and since it was a primary ordinance of his belief, he believed that he possessed the spirit of God and had the Gift. He also thought of himself as "God's gift to women," as the saying goes, and was articulate and good enough looking to sodomize and seduce more than one homely, usually young, but not exclusively teenage girls. His *modus operandi* included the line that he had been chosen by God as a healer and a prophet of good tidings; that whosoever had any kind of sex with him was thereby anointed and baptized in the spirit of the Lord. The acts of petting, foreplay, and ultimately intercourse—all were portrayed by him as spiritual, baptismal sacraments to the innocents who consented to his decadent, untoward advances.

When presented with the opportunity of a liaison with a more mature conquest he affectedly recited a few poems of seduction, inevitably modulating from the stories of the Virgin Mary, Delilah, Jezebel, and Bathsheba into Andrew Marvel's "To His Coy Mistress," or other Cavalier verses dealing with *carpe diem* and their need, really his, to "gather the rosebuds while ye may." One of his most effective approaches was ironically to offer his own brand of atonement, absolving his conquests of guilt, reinforcing the idea that a woman's lot was to follow and serve if not worship man. Moreover, he psychologically played upon his Faustian namesake, and what he considered his birthright to offer and to bestow salvation to sinner and believer alike by unburdening their souls of any collateral sins. Naturally, inevitably he had harmed more gullible women than he had benefited let alone "saved."

Few were aware of Faustine's carefully crafted persona or his padded, fraudulent résumé when called first to a revival and then to lead the Living Faith Assembly on the outskirts of Mountainair. The humble looking, unassuming if not rundown church had been without a preacher for several months, unable, as it were, to guarantee a satisfactory living wage and parsonage. The last preacher had insisted on often worshiping with rattlesnakes in his services, disillusioning most of the congregation by being bitten one Sunday and dying within a week.

Nina's father and uncle and two or three other members, in the interim, had tried to rid the church of any escaped or hidden snakes, keeping up the grounds, patching the roof and securing a crude cross atop the Narthex. The female membership, including Nina's mother and aunt dusted pews and mopped floors, covering the austere altar and sequestering incidental liturgical objects, including the pitchers and cups used in Holy Communion. Raul, when hoeing weeds, had almost been bitten by a large rattler. That one wound up losing its head in a shovel's flash.

Being a portly bachelor and essentially a ne'er-do-well, Faustine found what was offered in the remote post sufficient for a first fling at being a sanctioned preacher at a mission church, however meager. He'd been advised by his mentor, the reverend Benavidez, to make inroads into the youth of the community, confident that their parents would gladly follow, footing the bill, assured that church attendance was a bastion against drugs, alcohol, illicit sex, and overall corrupting worldliness.

§

After a "fingers-crossed" automobile journey south in a rattletrap old Suburban bought from Reverend Benny for two-hundred dollars, and getting a week's lodging at the Palomino Motel, Faustine's first full service at Living Faith, that auspicious fall Sunday morning when he was introduced to the congregation and to the Lucero family, Lalo, Linda, Rosendo and

Nina, Raul, his wife, Estelle, and two little girls as founding members and eminent land holders and sheep ranchers, Faustine started making plans on how to impress them and especially to captivate nubile Nina, whom he excitedly lusted for at first glance.

During his first sermon, which was chosen on what he guessed to be the germane story of Cain and Abel and the implications of fratricide and their respective offerings to Yahweh, he made a special point of looking as frequently as possible at the Lucero family. In reality he was not just seeming to but truly preaching at them. And his message of sacrifice, murder, guilt, sibling rivalry and the centrality of paternalism seemed to register with Rosendo and Nina who, slowly stopping their gum chewing, were almost hypnotized by Faustine's penetrating glare. Nina's mind wandered to her past violent violation by the Crawford brothers and her, "Was I asking for it?" guilt in feeling freed by the rape, ambivalently loathing but partially liking the attack and the "burden" of losing her virginity—a loss for her ironically modulating into a gain.

After the service the exiting receiving line became a procession of welcoming members, enthusiastic, albeit a bit cowed and beclouded by the imposing presence of the brash new preacher.

He approached the Luceros by asking a well planned and, admittedly, a researched favor, extending an obsequious hand and speaking first to Linda.

"Such a pleasure, Mrs. Lucero. I've heard about you and your family, of course, your work at the ruins, and your talented and hard-working family. I simply can't resist asking if you might introduce me to the Salinas ruins and the ancient worship history of the monument, most especially the padres."

Her answer was quick and sincere.

"But of course, Reverend. It would be my pleasure. Many friars over many years. We'll have you over for brunch and then visit at least one ruin. Their use as churches will of course especially interest you."

Lalo extended his calloused hand to clasp the fat-fingered young man and reinforced his wife's cordial invitation. "Welcome, Revered Medina. Yes, yes, please visit us and we'll show you our ranch and sheep operation, traceable again back to the history of the ruins in history, myth, and the raising of sheep in this area. A much prized and reverential animal in our biblical teachings, as you know."

"But of course, *a sus ordines,* please call me Fausto, sir. I have a sermon or two planned on Christ as the Good Shepard and the imagery of the blood of the lamb." Nodding and turning swiftly to Rosendo and Nina, the dark and roving-eyed, portly pastor extended his own oily-slick invitation.

"Young man," he said to Rosendo, "You must

play your guitar here in church. Word is that you are quite the talent."

And then to Nina: "How about enlisting your service here in the church young lady? I hear you are a cheerleader and honor society member and speak your mind. The Lord knows we can use your leadership abilities here. May I count on you?"

She smiled but slightly grimaced, in part because his handshake was unusually sweaty, squeezed then relaxed, and then again firm, augmented by what she felt as a slimy, stubby-fingered caress on her wrist—confirmed when he reached out to place his fumbling hand on her head—with the other one sliding ever so lightly across her chest.

§

The brunch was prepared and waiting, when Faustine's jalopy pulled into the long gravel driveway of the Lucero ranch house. He'd marveled at the miles of mesa and foothills and wide vista surrounding the place, framed easterly by the sublime Manzano mountain range, noting one particularly high peak, and was relieved when he finally located the crude but impressive ranch sign, hanging on a barbed wire fence aside a gate, saying simply "LUCERO" in bold, crudely-welded brass letters on a burnished steel plate.

"Some impressive spread," he thought and blew out a silent spittle whistle of approval into the shimmying steering wheel as he turned down the washboard road toward the big, stark cottonwood tree standing sentinel by the approaching rambling, tin-roofed, adobe house.

Parents, children, and a jacked up, jumping pair of border collies were quick to greet, then soon avoid the rotund pastor, decked out today in baggy jeans, an oversized belt buckle, Justin roper roughouts, and a worn but flamboyant Larry Mahan maroon, pearl-buttoned shirt with a fancy but frayed gray yoke, augmented by an apparently just purchased Carhartt vest. Clearly, he wanted to impress, notwithstanding his penury and a physique unfriendly to western wear.

"We hoped you could find us," Linda spoke first, saying in a slightly peeved tone, "Thank the Lord! Welcome, pastor. Brunch is ready."

Lalo piped up in a baritone hello, "*Bien venidos, Señor* Fausto. *Nuestro casa es su casa.* Come right this way," and he led him into the house following his wife and trailed by Rosendo and behind him a rather lackadaisical acting Nina.

Faustine turned politely and said to Nina and her brother, "*Pasa ustedes*—after you guys, "*Con su permiso, el viejo atras la hermasilla y el guapo!*" And he reached out for Nina's hand which she reluctantly extended in a loose, only somewhat tender finger grip.

Linda had prepared yucca-root iced tea, *biscochitos*, *natillas*, mincedmeat *empañadas*, and personally harvested and canned apricot jam.

Conversation centered around the church and Faustine's hopes for building its future, his interest in its reptilian past—and his reading about and growing curiosity in the Spanish missions once active and now in nearby ruins and in view of hypnotic mountains.

When he asked for a bit more ice in his tea Linda went to the kitchen, reached for her well used, familiar stag-handled ice pick, fashioned for her by Lalo, and forcefully cracked more ice from the twenty-five-pound block still in the sink, placing the ice pick back in its standard resting place. Then in hurried steps she went back to serve her guest. Having his ice, Faustine, just as hurriedly dismissed her without so much as a thank you for his hostess. She, in her goodness, chalked it up to an oversight rather than rudeness.

Lalo told of his sheep and of the long enduring family tradition of his grandfather and great grandfather—Luceros who had once a century ago kept sheep in and around the ruins, grazing around the adjacent stream—part of his inheritance and present flock of 185 fine wool *Rambouillet* sheep, and destined to be his legacy too, his bequests to brother Raul, and Nina and Rosendo.

Rosendo brought out his beloved Mexican guitar with its abalone inlays and roseate purfling, and honored a request, after some noodling settling on a simplified but recognizable version of a Villa Lobos prelude in E minor.

"*Aplauso, joven, Qué Bueno! Gracias amigo, Muchos Gracias, muchisimo!*" Faustine clapped and loudly shouted in an ingratiating but embarrassing "Hurrah"! "We must arrange for a concert at the church as soon as possible."

Nina was applauding too when asked by the preacher, "And you...most beautiful sister and daughter, what are your hobbies and talents, my dear, other than bestow sunshine wherever you are?" He looked her over, in effect undressing her head to toe, dwelling on her large, rough looking hands, and soft, blue-veined neck—her long, unruly but beautiful blonde hair, and the contour of her lovely, young and pliant breasts.

"I raise livestock to show at the State Fair, and I'm studying self-defense, hoping to major in physical therapy at *Tomé* or Hobbs or CNMC and become a physical trainer and expert in mixed martial arts.

I know how to fight somewhat effectively even now, thanks to my uncle. In school I'm a cheerleader and I like history and P.E."

"Well, yes, your reputation as one who speaks her mind and can defend herself precedes you, according to some of the young church members who've mentioned you to me."

Soon they were off to visit Quarai, the closest of the missions though not the largest. Lalo begged off, saying he needed to stay and tend to chores, but Linda enthusiastically drove there, exited the car and guided them, heading first to the publicity rack to orient Faustine with pamphlets and books, introducing him to the nearby docent, while Rosendo and Nina began wandering through the various vacant and eerie portions of the ruin.

Linda excused herself to talk business with her colleague, telling Faustine to go ahead and explore the place. He soon caught up with Nina, nervously reaching out his arms to hold her by both hands and saying the most surprising, mind-blowing thing she had ever heard or expected to hear.

"Dearest Nina, I must tell you precious one that the Lord has mystically spoken to me and directed me to take you as my wife together to lead the host of local lost souls to salvation. I am like Christ a divinely chosen good shepherd who has been led here to this ancient sacred spot and to declare you the destined, chosen little lamb of godly love. By and in Christ's blood and crucifixion you are to be my found and rescued lost lamb of peace and in me find atonement and forgiveness of your wayward, sinful, guilty, promiscuous past in which you were immersed. I have learned this in a revelation. It has been revealed that your name 'Nina' is meant to rhyme with 'Medina.'"

And before she could shut her wide open, shocked, totally flabbergasted mouth and loosen herself from him, he began babbling incoherent sounds like guttural groans and slobbering stuttering all in search of some semblance of sense. She stood in shock witnessing him descend deeper into the possession of his trance, seemingly channeling all the ancient spirits, Native American, Hispanic, or Anglo of every ghost or incubus ever haunting, living and dying at this uncanny locale, finally ending with the abstruse statement, "*En este mundo no hay sitio para mi ruinas.*"

LOS CASADOS

Nina was young, only in her teens and compliant, naive and believing in her pastor, in the beginning, but she'd had a hard time adjusting to what she was convinced were Faustine's perversions of holy matrimony, which he said he had deduced from scripture. They had a small parsonage apartment close to the church—a disappointing living arrangement for Nina who missed her room at the ranch and all her barnyard friends.

The first major wrinkle in the relationship, however, came when Faustine insisted on Nina giving up her dream of showing *El Chingón* Billy *El Gruff* at the State Fair, insisting that he would make a great meal offered up in sacrificial homage to the Lord. Not unlike, in his mind, the miracle of Christ serving wine, bread, and fishes.

They could roast the goat in a pit at the church and use that burnt-offering event to celebrate the infusion of new life in the living but languishing faith of Living Faith's dwindling congregation. It took some persuading and arguing that it would secure Nina's place among the angels of the Lord. "Proof, my dear, that your love for me is lordly and supreme," was the way he put it.

She didn't like the subservience, taking that profound, heart-rending order and other lesser quotidian orders; and the doughy touch, sticky embrace of Faustine's soon recognized as disturbing, if not disgusting, love making; and being at his beck and call—his obesity; his come-hither hand gestures and his whinny voice; his flatulence and incoherent gibberish when ordering his food as if she were an entranced clairvoyant waitress in a desolate diner, or some spaced-out short order cook. His was always a monotonous weekly Sunday breakfast of bacon and eggs with green chile; and having his coffee at just the right temperature; then there were his corny jokes about her needing to be like Goldie Locks, getting things "just right, not too hot and not too cold" for Papa Bear.

More than once she longed for the now self-induced orgasmic passion occasioned in dreams of the Crawford twins, her legs forced apart there in the barn hay, while staring into *Cabrón* Billy's baleful eyes.

Just why Faustine insisted on intercourse first thing on Sunday morning, toasted with grape juice, soon became repulsive to say the least. He insisted that it helped him compose his sermon, a session always announced by "Let us pray and give unto the Lord," and requesting that she appear in nothing more than a Victoria's Secret apron at the breakfast table. An apron he'd had modified with the words "God is Love" embroidered across the front, "God" in front of one breast, "Love" in front of the other one, an apron he ritualistically and roughly removed before nestling between her resentful breasts and awkwardly taking her on the hard, back-breaking kitchen counter—or the "altar of love" as he called it, always obliquely muttering about the ending of Steinbeck's *The Grapes of Wrath* and "Rosasharn, Rosasharn," Rose of Sharon, causing Nina to check out the book in town, identify with the character's mysteries of motherhood but sorely resent Faustine's profane appropriation of the character.

§

Nina's own pregnancy followed and then a second one followed that and before Nina could fully realize it, the blessing and burden of birth and the time involved in taking care of two small boys, plus the church responsibilities of being the preacher's wife, she was exhausted and depressed, drowning in delayed postpartum blues, fueled by regret and guilt at how she had let her life get out of control—out of her control, but under her domineering husband's.

She'd confided in her father who reinforced the teaching that husbands led and wives followed, and that the family was honored by her wifely position in the church. Her more understanding mother, still carrying a grudge for Faustine's gauche, continuing ill manners, suggested she seek the help of a chiropractor who had helped Linda with physical therapy when in pain. That registered with Nina who had long given up on her dream of getting a degree or at least a certificate in some kind of physical or occupational therapy. So she searched and found the phone number of Doctor Clyde Renfrow in the Albuquerque directory and made an appointment, telling Faustine, truthfully enough, that it was for her back ache.

She left Eduardo and Eloy, her little boys, with her mother and asked Raul if he or Estelle would drive her to her appointment. Estelle agreed and soon Nina was in Renfro's office on his elaborate motorized table with him elevating her on her head and then lowering her, pulling her legs from the ankles and telling her she needed to avoid back-straining activities and, at least for a few weeks, not to lift more than twenty-five pounds, drink more water, and join a gym, preferably with a personal trainer. "Get some really good shoes too," he added.

"I have a friend, Anthony Arruejo, a Filipino young man who's well versed in his country's martial arts, especially Malay and knife fighting, but he also knows jujitsu, even some Krav Maga; ironically, he knows relaxation techniques and he's certified as a personal trainer. Tony just opened a "Get Fit" store and gym in a small strip mall on the corner of West Central and Parkway, Eighth and Parkway to be exact, on the south side of the road—just east of Washington school. It's not far from Old Town.

In offering further testimonial to Arruejo, Renfro said, "He was stationed at Kirtland in the Air Force as an MP and decided to stay and set up business. He's a jovial fellow even in a fight and has started offering classes to enhance strength and flexibility and foster self-defense skills as well as relaxation and mindfulness—techniques culled from his many studies. Look for the symbol of the Malay triangle on the door. I'll get you his card up front."

Such a teacher qualified in multiple forms of self-defense and relaxation both stymied and appealed to Nina thinking it would be somewhat of a drive, maybe once a week, but she was pretty much at wit's end and knew she had to do something, so why not this?

"Plenty to choose from," she chuckled to herself in her husky voice! "Just call me 'Grasshopper, a silly Queenie Kung Fu,'" thinking of David Carradine's hokey television show. "Maybe I can convince Raul or Estelle, or even dad to drive me. Besides, it's time I had the courage to drive myself into the city."

§

A couple of days back home, and one afternoon between house-keeping, meal-making, a swollen-eyed crying spell, and a bruise on her arm occasioned by being grabbed by Faustine, Nina retrieved the business card Renfro had given her and called the "Get Fit" number.

A young-sounding voice with a slight accent answered, saying, "Welcome, we're here to condition you for a happier life and to reclaim your physical and psychological strength. 'Readiness is all,' we too say."

"Hello sir. What are your membership plans?

A Mr. Clyde Renfro referred me to you. My name is Nina Lucero, I mean Lucero-Medina. I'm twenty-two years old, a house wife, wanting to learn more about fighting to protect myself and in need of more strength more stamina to help me do daily activities."

"Yes, but . . . certainly. This is Anthony, the owner." She could tell his voice had an air of happiness in it.

"Yes, my friend Mr. Renfro—I helped him in the past when I was at the base; he told me of you. Do you want the full, twice a week, personal trainer, two-hundred dollars; or the partial, once-a-week, one hundred-dollar group plan?"

After a few more details Nina chose the once-a-week plan and enrolled for the classes beginning in the new year. "*Vamos a ver*," she said.

"*Seguro, señora*," he said. "*Si, si*! We will see."

§

It took some persuasion and the enlistment of her relatives to convince a reluctant, increasingly moody Faustine that the fitness class was needed and affordable. But they came to her defense and argued that given her present lackadaisical behavior, edginess and sallow look, she needed some kind of elixir and this structured class in martial arts seemed to fit the bill.

"She's been watching too much television, disinterested in the boys, in church duties and obviously needs to get stronger. She's always been interested in fighting at school and on TV. This diversion might help," Linda said.

Lalo said, "I'll pay the fees. No worries there. It's a small thing, Faustine. We can drive her. She can drive my truck. No worries."

Raul and Estelle agreed to do the driving to and from the big city, while Rosendo coughed and said with a slur, "She deserves a break, man. Let her go."

And so it was decided. She'd go. She'd grow stronger and learn meditation and martial arts. But first she had to get through the holidays, and that would mean work and travail. Even some grief, no doubt. The holiday blues and blahs. Service at the church. A nativity scene. Decorations. Food. Presents. Emotions! She would ask Rosendo for more marijuana if he would share it. That would be a sibling perk for moving back to the ranch. Plus mom would help watch the boys. Then there's Rosendo and his smoky guitar. He's been staying in his room, singing less and stingy too—worried more about getting caught lately," she continued to muse.

Feliz Navidad

November...and holidays were upon them again and old traditions revived. Time for the fall deer hunt around Manzano Peak. Raul was again the organizer. It meant setting up a camp and a tent. Carting groceries. Lalo, feeling the holiday spirit, wanted to invite Faustine too this year but Raul demurred, finally giving in, saying "Just so that *guajolote* doesn't mistake anybody for a buck or a gobbler, okay! But you'll have to loan him a gun. You know when it comes to nimrods or nitwits, my guns are my guns!" So the date was set for the second week before Thanksgiving. If luck held sway they would have success *prontisimo.*

Linda, Nina, Estelle, and Raul's new girlfriend, Yvonne, would help with gathering supplies, especially groceries; however, they would stay behind and work on home and hearth, ranch, homes, and getting the church up to spec—the church nativity and decorations ready for display right after Thanksgiving.

Nina volunteered to pick out the best ewe for the display, and block out a schematic for the positions of the manger, the sheep, Joseph, Mary, the Wise Men, and baby Jesus. The same large doll used in past years would be the star, although chipped, faded, and generally the worse for wear. Those items were stored in the church utility room, along with costumes, fake beards, robes, staffs, and such.

While the women took their inventory, the men turned to armament and camp supplies: the old Sears tent, the Coleman stove and lanterns, the sleeping bags and air mattresses, the camouflage clothing, the guns and the ammunition.

Lalo invited the pesky reverend Fausto and he agreed to go after only a slight hesitation. "*Seguro*, Lalo, I've never hunted deer before but I can tag along, enjoy the scenery and maybe cook some meals. Any prayers needed and I'll be there."

They arrived at the camp spot, at the base of the highest peak in the Manzano range, late in the afternoon, and under Raul's direction unloaded supplies and set up the tent. The pines smelled beautiful and the air was invigorating. The aspens waved to them from on high. Hunger soon set in, so naturally the next order of business was supper. There too Raul took control. He instructed Rosendo to gather the wood and build a campfire, done in short order just as twilight began to engulf them.

Supper was a satisfying combination of ground round steak, sliced potatoes, onions, and baked beans, the Coleman stove performed up to expectations. Beer was the prevailing beverage although Rosendo and Faustine opted for a cold Coke. Lalo settled himself in a comfortable folding "Sportsman" reclining chair, retrieving a cigarette, lighting it with a well-chosen flaming twig from the fire. Rosendo gathered the tin plates and entered the tent to arrange the cots and bedrolls. Faustine started talking about how impressed he was by the mountains, the Ruins and the history of the area around the ranch, asking rather vapid questions about state involvement in restoration, benefactors, wills, donations, benevolences, Spanish padres, Apaches, sheep and the women in the Living Faith congregations. He tried an off-color joke about hot tamales, and soon was found scraping his boot toe in the black dirt at his feet.

Lalo didn't say much, mostly puffed on his Camel cigarette, listening and thinking about what might be the motives behind so many odd, inappropriate, unconnected questions, and suddenly feeling deep sorrow for his daughter.

Raul opened another can of Coors, stroked his goatee, and began unzipping gun cases, checking the rifles, saying to Fausto that he'd be carrying a loaned, rusty, old 300 Savage lever action, showing him some of its features, especially how to load and unload it; but most of all the location of the safety.

"You'll have to be very careful, preacher, and never point this in our direction. It can kill not just a deer but one of us—or yourself! I understand you've never hunted or carried a rifle before...no military background, right?

"Oh, don't worry about me," he said, lipping his reply into his still half-full Coke can. I've read about biblical weaponry, about Joshua and Esau and David and Goliath, and Samson too with his trusty jawbone of an ass. I've taken notes about all kinds of threats—animal, vegetable, or mineral. I'm gifted with certain innate smarts and invincibility."

"My ass! *Chingada!*" Raul said out loud, a remark drawing laughs and hoots from the others, including Lalo who exhaled a smoky editorial, "Animals ain't read no Bible."

§

Raul was the first up the next morning rustling

everyone out of their bedrolls, already having the coffee made. When they were fully dressed and awake he recommended which direction they should take and how they should pair off. He would go with Rosendo, and Lalo and the preacher would hunt together.

The morning sun was hitting the earth and steam could be seen drifting upwards from the moist tree tops. Lalo insisted walking behind Fausto, nervous about the neophyte's way with the rifle. He had to whisper to him not to huff and puff and to breathe more softly. Even Lalo could smell the preacher's sweat, thinking, "*Diablos!*, They'll smell him downwind."

Trying to be tactful Lalo advised, "You take it easy fella. You're really out of condition. Just walk slower and I'll adjust my pace. We're in no hurry. "*Esto no es una carrera, hombre.*"

Raul asked Rosendo if he was clear headed, saying "*queremos no vatos loco hoy,* chapito." The young man laughed and guaranteed he was hitting on all cylinders and ready to down a big buck.

The two groups were only one canyon apart, but still far from the crest of the ten-thousand feet peak. The hope was that any deer one party scared up would maybe run across the plateau to the other. There were plenty of fresh signs, prints of hooves and droppings—the day transforming into one of clear azure skies and cold but not freezing wind.

Closer to the head of their respective canyons Lalo was shocked to see Faustine jerk and quickly raise his gun to his shoulder, firing wildly into some brush and awkwardly levering another shell in the chamber. "Boom! Another shot rang out, then another, Wham! And yet a third...Carraranggg!"

Lalo held his ears, now ringing from such close firing. "*Chingada tu madre hombre, que pasa, a que disparas, Burro!*"

Faustine yelled, "A devil turkey, *Viejo*, didn't you hear it gobble sounds of damnation? I think I got him. I shot right where he was. One dead demon turkey *por dios!*

"*Idiota,* Lalo said. It isn't turkey season *Buey* and that sound was no damn turkey! That was a squirrel barking. *Una ardilla no es un guajolote, como tu!*"

"Just joking, Viejo," Faustine quickly backfilled his bizarre excuse, blaming it to magic, "It shape-shifted into a devil deer; didn't you see that big rack, those huge flaming horns and nostrils? I did. I had to shoot. Had to save us!"

Lalo stopped in his tracks wondering what in heaven or hell had come upon the poor minister!

Raul and Rosendo, hearing the three shots, turned back and headed for the camp. "Maybe they got one. Maybe it's trouble. Three shots mean help," uttered Raul. "Let's go see," Rosendo said, already winded, striking out in a run.

§

The Thanksgiving table was plentiful with food of every sort, most of it enhanced by either green or red chile. There was a large-breasted hen turkey, of course, but the imaginary turkey become creature Fausto said he saw and shot was the main course—and the dessert of ridicule and humor.

"Faustine's turkey venison isn't very filling. Pass me another slice of that real turkey with real dressing and gravy; I'll pass on the spirit lamb chop." Rosendo joked. "Add a piece of heavenly pie alamode while you're at it."

Not only was Faustine's nightmare turkey missing at the table but soon so was Faustine. He'd been razzed into returning to his small apartment, holding up and saying he had to get busy getting Christmas lined up at the church.

Nina was more at odds with him now than ever and not only embarrassed for him but ashamed that he had become the brunt of her family's jokes. She had teased him before only to feel the back of his hand strike her across the face. She retaliated by throwing every piece of crockery she could find in the cupboard. He lost more than he gained by such abuse. She retreated back to the ranch, welcoming solace from her mother but mostly regret and some blame from her father for marrying this prominent *pirujo,* such a disappointment as a man, and as the congregation was discovering, a pathetic preacher, loco church leader and all-around jackass.

Nina, however, had promised to help with the Nativity scene and the Christmas Eve service. With her planning and eye for symmetry and distance perspective, things were coming together nicely. She had the lamb, actually two pet lambs selected and had even arranged to borrow a donkey and a docile milk cow. There would be no want of animals. She had all the Wise Men cast, chosen from distant relatives and close by friends. Even the Crawford boys relented and embarrassingly agreed to participate, albeit now only partially "forgiven."

Fake beards, robes and staffs were in supply although a bit moth-eaten from improper storage. Everything was subject to either washing or airing out to regain some of its luster.

Rosendo had practiced and practiced "Silent Night," "Ave Maria," and "Away in a Manger" and was ready with three beautifully harmonized versions.

When it came to his beloved guitar he was a true believer, encouraged too by Yvonne who found him, as she said, "dreamy-eyed," offering to sing with him if he wanted.

So the Nativity was set up in front of the church, the animals secure in place on Christmas Eve. The display was praised by all who saw it—non-members too—bringing much praise and pride to Nina for near perfection. Then when all the players were dressed in their clean wardrobes and combed, pasty beards they paraded across the altar. Baby Jesus, now in the arms of Mary, played by Yvonne, was the closest thing to a living child any doll could be. The music portion was ready and Rosendo played "Silent Night" with a Latin beat as the congregation was seated, just before Faustine's Christmas message. Rosendo was scheduled to play again after the benediction.

When Faustine stepped up to the candle-lit pulpit to comment on the meaning of Christmas, and the birth of the Christ child, the mood, however, began to change with the flickering, smoke ascending from the giant, pine-scented Nambe *La Luz* candles brought by tonight's guest, come down from that small native town with other "gifts," Faustine pointing in an arm-waving gesture to the curious, large, wriggling towsack placed next to the altar.

"Folks, God bless you and me and all those

individuals and families who believe," Faustine began. "I, of course, include my hard-working wife and our two little boys, seated right there in front with their mother. My mother-in-law and father-in-law and other in-laws are here too and we are all blessed by their support, tithes and devoted work for the church.

Tonight is a special night of birth and blessing. Baby Jesus whose effigy rests behind me now in its mother's arms and in our players, leaving our modeled manger and a sacred Nativity "Inn" which give Him rest and honor and acknowledgement of his birthright. Tonight's message is a forward looking one, a message of gratitude for the possibilities of forgiveness of our sins and atonement offered by the one who took on all our transgressions and burdens and sacrificed his life for our salvation if we only believe in him, have faith and carry on his name preaching the spirit of baptism in his spirit, the spirit of the Son, the Father, and the Holy Ghost!

"I have faith that the spirit of the Lord is here, in this church, this very night where the eternal battle with Satan will be dramatized tonight thanks to my mentor and spiritual father, the right reverend Benjamin Benavidez, who is visiting with us tonight from Farmington and bringing his Christmas gifts, the gifts of faith, of belief in scripture, and the eternal life and cleansing which that offers.

"Can I hear an *"Amen"* brothers and sisters? A thankful, believing *"Amen"*? Yes, yes, that's what I want to hear. *Amen! Amen! Amen*! I bring you the Word and you hear, having Faith in my words, faith in the Word, faith in the Reverend Ben's words you are about to hear and see and experience deep in your soul.

"First, however, let me offer a homily, a parable, a story of my recent encounter with evil and my quick reaction in its face. Deep in the wilderness, amidst the heavy brush of the Manzano mountains I was deer hunting near the highest peak, *Ustedes sabes*? (You know. . . where the aspens begin), with my relatives the very ones seated in front here tonight. Suddenly a demonic vision appeared to me. Not unlike Satan's temptation of Christ on that biblical mountain, said to be Mount Quarantania in Matthew's account.

"It was Lucifer incarnate, fallen from grace, with the head of a serpent and the cloven feet of the immortal Devil. At first it appeared as a deer but the horns, yes, the very antlers of the spirit deer soon took on the shape of serpents, waving and weaving and hissing like a mythical Medusa. In a flash I raised my gun and shot three quick (Father-Son-Holy-Ghost) shots in His name and the egregious visage disappeared! When I went to look...yes when I went to look, do you know what I found, people? Do you know? Can you imagine? *Sabes*? *Una milagro grande*!

Yes, it was a two-headed serpent and I had shot him through the eyes. Believe as I do, brothers and sisters, Believe!"

The congregation began to move and to moan in the pews and say "Believe! Believe! We believe!" Lalo and Linda, Raul and Estelle, sensing something wasn't right, too began to grow restless, demonstrating a kind of body shaking heebie-jeebies. Nina and Rosendo sat still although gesticulating and twitching their faces as if stricken with some kind of involuntary neurological tic. Rosendo clutched his guitar, holding it to his pounding chest, seeking a sympathetic vibration! The two little boys, Eddie and Eloy, huddled closer and closer to their mother, stopping their scribbling on offering envelopes.

Faustine was now waving his arms and stomping his feet and yelling out "Praise Him! Praise the Lord! He cometh! He is *con nosotros* here tonight. *Contigo! Contigo*! We can feel him. He is inside us, our hearts and souls. Feel him! Feel him! Brethren He is here! Sisters, He is with us again tonight on the eve of his birth! Believe! Believe!"

He interrupted his flailing and antsy, jitterbug steps to say, "Benny! Benny! *Ahora, compadre! Ahora*! The time is here. Come unto us here and administer your offering. The hour has come! Midnight! *Hora majica! La hora de las hechicinas! las brujas*!

A thin, stooped, bearded man shuffled to the front from a side pew. He too was waving his arms and hopping around and he first went to the back of the church then skipped and hollered up the central aisle to the altar where he picked up the towsack and waved it about this head, allowing the snakes inside to fall out in a twisted, writhing knot, one slithering down Benny's humped back.

He grabbed the wriggling sphere of reptiles and shook it as if straightening out a knot of electrical cords, screaming, "Get thee hence, get thee behind me devils!" finally securing one just behind its head, its long, extended tongue waving like a baton in rhythm to its beautifully scaly-patterned, hypnotically dangling body.

The other snakes slid away in different directions, sliding under the pulpit and any object they could find, any exit away from the noise and commotion. One or two moved out into the congregation cascading over stairs and curving around tables, causing most or the here-to-fore sceptics and those remembering the death of the previous spiritual snake-charmer pastor, to run shaking for the doors.

"Calmaté gente, calmaté!" Benny shouted. Faustine had the temerity to pick up another snake and let it wrap itself around his shoulder and neck, saying, "*Wunderbar, wunderbar! Die schlange ist konig!*"

taking the snake's head and placing it next to his face, as if daring it to strike, taking another one and trying to stuff it in his breast pocket like a handkerchief.

Soon most of the people were outside lined up and kicking their feet high in the air as if doing some country-western *Can-can* to Jerry Lee Lewis's "Whole Lot of Shakin' Going On."

Most didn't notice that the Reverend Benny was bitten on the cheek, and Faustine had to pull the snake's fangs away from his neck. Such was their faith that they believed the only antidote needed was faith. Such was the assertion of Benny, who with Faustine headed straight to the Sheriff's department for an escort to the city hospital—antivenom shots supporting their faith.

Lalo and Linda swept their family away (Nina and Rosendo and the boys riding with Raul and Estelle), peeled out and Raul too tore onto the gravel road, rolling blind, and only turning on the headlights a half mile down the main highway back to the ranch, Nina screaming "That man, that "*pinche* preacher wannabe husband" is crazy. *Poco loco y mas*! *Tengo miedo*! He scares me shitless! I've had it with him!"

El Gimnasio

After New Year's, early in January, Raul and Estelle dropped Nina off in a mall in front of a rather small West side cubbyhole business designated "Get Fit" in large serif letters painted purple and black over the doorway of number 806 Parkway. Between the two main words in the double-outlined business name was a stylized shape of a barbell. A small neon sign blinked "Open" in red. A large black triangle decal shown through the front-door glass.

Seeing several people moving inside, she waved goodbye to Raul and Estelle, pointing to her wrist and holding up fingers and mouthing the number "Nine" to reinforce the communication. She then opened the heavy glass door.

There were about a dozen people inside, mostly men, some swinging kettle bells and a couple of guys shadow boxing. A muscular woman was doing pushups and a friend talking to her was busy doing rows on the TRX. A rather anorexic elderly large-bosomed lady with bulgy, scared knees, bleached blonde scraggly hair, and crepe paper skin was attempting to peddle a stationary bicycle. Over in a back corner an elderly, distinguished-looking, silver-headed gentleman was arm wrestling a big bruiser of an Irishman. The place had the sweet, rancid smell of sweat.

Nina did a double take when she thought she recognized Jenny "*Wisa*" Duran and Martha "Titty-tats" Jimenez from school. "How the hell could they be here?" she said to herself and started to turn around and leave, not knowing if it was Jenny or the people or the stations and devices which intimidated her the most. But she refused to be cowed, shrugged her shoulders, took off her coat and gawked some more, waiting to be recognized herself, soon to be greeted by a handsome Eurasian man dressed in a black and white-striped Adidas warmup suit.

He was tall, olive complexioned, and had a thin, rather sad-looking goatee but a full head of thick, long, glistening black hair tied in a top-knot—in contrast with closely-cropped hair over his temples and ears.

His eyes reminded her of Navajo eyes. Real ones and the ones on the back of Navajo Freight Line trucks.

"Greetings and welcome, Miss. I'm Anthony, or Tony if you will, the owner. And you must be Miss or rather Mrs. Nina Lucero Medina, the friend of my old friend Clyde, Hang Five, Renfro. Glad you could make it. We'll start in just a few minutes, but feel free to warm up."

Nina didn't know what the surfer aside meant and couldn't tell if her heart was fluttering out of fright or delight with the looks and presence of this striking young man, so much better looking than Faustine or any boy she'd ever had a crush on. "He's a dream, she thought. A living dream!" She had never met any Asian, and was a bit biased against them, given Raul's war stereotypes he'd fostered in Vietnam. This man, however, looked Anglo too, and was captivating.

Fantasy soon overtook her, forgetting all about her now bug-eyed schoolmates, and imagined what it would be like to make love with this, this "Anthony-Tony" fellow.

"Okay gang!" he shouted. "Everybody over here and let's get started. Around the horn first for introductions. Names, goals, comments."

Come Nina's turn she spoke up loudly, looking at Jenny and Martha and simply saying "I want to get stronger and fight better if I have to. Plus . . . I want a kind of peace."

Others said much the same thing although the hefty woman who had been doing pushups announced that she and her friend Lucy intended to enter a weight lifting competition in the spring.

The crepe-paper skinned *vieja* straw-headed blonde announced that she "wanted to learn how to 'hoochy-kootchie' in the back seat of my Mercedes, the way the kids do it," obviously mistaking that term, maybe, for a Japanese martial art or so Anthony hoped, guiltily dreading working with her.

Jenny and Martha dramatically resurrected the crippling *Mal de Ojo*, saying they were here "to deliver" and jumped into a high five followed by a couple of hard but rippling hip bumps.

The session was mostly directed toward increasing flexibility, starting with upper body shoulder rolls and arm extensions above and behind the head. Anthony explained some rudimentary anatomical terminology as to core, triceps, biceps, pectorals; then leg muscles, listing quadriceps, hamstrings, *gluteus maximus*, calves, and the like, interrupting the overview by humorously singing about how the foot bones were connected to the ankle bones, to the leg bones, the hip bones and ultimately the brain bone.

They all laughed and groaned at his attempt at humor and dismissed into the night. Except for Nina. Anthony continued saying that he would teach anyone some Filipino martial arts if interested, cautioning them of the potential deadliness of certain moves and holds. He hoped also to impart some meditation techniques. Even diet, which was of crucial importance.

She was stopped at the coat rack by Anthony for a brief few words of inspiration, confirming in short, "You can do this and I'm here to help you." He hesitated a second and then said, "Do you know those two girls here to 'deliver' like they said? I thought I noticed some hostile glances.

We can work on taming that down too. We can do it through fighting, ironically. You'll leave here friends after I schedule some team work."

Nina virtually glowed as she walked out into the night to meet Raul and Estelle and get into their toasty Chevy—the red dirt of the mountain roads stull needing to be washed off.

Nina, concerned that they had been inconvenienced asked, "*Qué pasa*? How did you guys make it? "Oh, we just shopped down in Old Town, watched the luminarias, looked at decorations still up. Walked around *Plaza Vieja*."

When they asked her "How did it go?" All she could say was, "He was just great! *Muy suave*. So very kind!" Then she shuddered, making a mental note to ask her mother to fashion a spell-breaking charm for her before next week. How could it really be coincidence seeing them there?

Then she thought, but didn't really care, "Faustine won't understand anything about this: my new joy! my new life! Maybe that snakebite is yet to kill the insane bastard. Whatever happens, however, he'll be mad—and the boys and I will pay the price."

§

Nina was right. Faustine didn't like what he heard in reports, rumors, real and imagined, (started in part by Jenny and Martha) about her new "GOOD GUY" trainer and her fitness goals—wanting to be a trainer herself and learning more about martial arts!

"Bologna. Bullshit, *Qué bofa!*, we'll see about that!" Those thoughts were Faustine's black summations, saying to her, "You're wasting good money on vanity, on so called self-improvement. Might as well call it "selfish" improvement. Spend that money and time with your children, and with me! To hell with you, Nina! Spend more time with church doings. You're going to the devil straight away woman. Straight away!"

Linda and Lalo grew even more concerned at the rift in their daughter's marriage but sided with her now more than they had. The two grandchildren were now considered theirs not just to baby sit but to protect. Their son-in-law, in growing more estranged was growing more deranged, hardly making any sense at all in his sermons. Known around the small town for roaming the streets, talking to himself, preaching on corners with bible in hand, throwing tantrums and exhibiting hostility to local sales clerks. Even the mechanics who worked on keeping his jalopy in minimum running order had complained to Jesus Baca, their boss, and to other customers. Some said he was seen circling the church at night, waving a long knife, yelling and cursing at demons shouting incantations: *"Ven aqui serpientes! Ven aqui culebras malditos, ven aqui, ven aqi"* As a result, the congregation was increasingly drifting away in larger numbers as the weeks went by. Not that there were that many members to begin with. Any attrition was considered catastrophic, but the scare of the Christmas Eve snake ceremony terrified most of the long-standing elderly members who now thought of church worship as a circus act. And the preacher— well, they surmised, had been poisoned by madness.

Nina couldn't let Faustine's disturbing antics deter her. Rather that become terrified or let guilt consume her, she resolved to exercise more, to strive for harder workouts, push herself to more sets of free weights, more reps of squats, more minutes on the treadmill and spinning on the bikes. Anthony had paired her with Jenny and Martha more than once on the TRX and punching bag and they were now sweating and conversing with one another.

Nina had even begun to drive herself to the gym in her father's pickup, never worried about darkness as the days turned longer with the seasonal change into spring.

Anthony was amazed at her determination, and into the last week of March he celebrated her birthday with a new set of kettle bells and a carton of trademarked "Powered Power" energy drinks of his own naming and devising.

She laughed at the comedy of the gifts. But it was a captivating laugh, an erotic laugh. And not really to her surprise he threw caution to the wind, told her he thought the world of her—embracing her, and kissing her like she'd never been kissed.

His kiss became her kiss and she willingly kissed him back, knowing bone deep that she would soon divorce Faustine who now meant little to her other than being the father of her children. She would get the divorce. Take the boys and move to Albuquerque to be with Anthony and together she was sure they could build up the gym into a thriving business. She knew, she felt, in that sustained and sustaining kiss those plans were now, in that moment well within her reach.

That night as she drove the hour-long trip on the back roads to the ranch, the fresh air flowing through the window wing vent in the truck, smelled sweeter than sweet, a mixture of mountain foliage and mesa sage, blending to enhance the music coming over the radio, a song by the Eagles singing "Peaceful Easy Feeling." And she fantasized about sleeping with Anthony that very night in the desert "with a billion stars all around."

April was coming. A new, promising spring. And she could start over. She could be herself!

La Lucha y La Fuga

When Faustine was asked to sign the divorce papers all hell broke loose and what residual sanity was left in his overwrought brain vanished. He jumped into his old Suburban and, clunking and rattling, headed for the ranch in a cloud of black exhaust. The route that had once been so enchanting for him was now a voyage through the wasteland, with first one scourge and then another attacking his thoughts.

He saw ghosts and indigenous spirits on the right and left of the highway and coming down the median to engulf him. It wasn't just the Lucero clan with whom he would have to do battle, it was the place, symbolized by the deterioration and disrepair of the ruins, year upon year, people upon people, failure upon failure, death upon death, burial upon burial—all piling up their sins and sickness, their betrayals and sins.

The ruins were a hell on earth with their long

shadows of desperation and departure, days upon days, months upon months, years upon years, decades upon decades, centuries upon centuries—those haunting and haunted ruins represented his own ruination, his own hopes and dreams theft, his destruction and death as surely as if a horde of renegade Apaches had scalped and ripped away his very soul; as surely as a troop of drunken marauders had ravaged him, drawing and quartering him; as surely as if he'd been staked to a mesa cactus for a horde of rattlesnakes to flood him with their venom harvested from the, synchronic satanic serpent, the eternal snake in the Garden which had caused the fall of Adam, of Eve, and of all mankind.

It had been encroaching on him since his arrival in this godless place: over in the Manzanos, inside the church, and now gorging and poisoning his brain. He would offer a sacrificial offering. His sons. He would kidnap his sons and make haste to the ruins and there perform a repellant ritual of dark atonement. He would be Abraham and they would be Isaac twice over; they would be a latter-day Cain and Abel and in both dying cleanse their fratricidal legacy.

In a manic maze he sped on through the night and pictured himself as Christ in the Judean desert being tempted by Satan. First on a parapet, then a peak overlooking the entire world. Biblical passages flashed before him, his synapses periodically shorting out and fizzling. Time stood still and rather than being behind the shaking steering wheel of his old panel truck he was beyond time, outside of reality and immersed in myth and murder.

The nearby ruins came into his mind. There he imagined the very parapet where Christ did battle with Satan and where James, Jesus's brother, was thrown down in execution. And beyond that the mountain peak where all dominions of the world were offered to Christ.

Faustine repeated to himself in a frantic liturgy "If I make it to the ruins and then the mountain I too will be an overlord." He rationalized that out of his evil acts good would come. He would be immortalized.

§

Linda and Nina were in the kitchen preparing lunch for the boys and for Lalo, who was out with the sheep checking on the possibility of foot rot—an ailment that hit his herds before, and which he thought he had recently smelled its foul odor returning. If confirmed, he would have to remove the infected ones from the herd before it spread.

Eloy was acting up and pestering his whining brother by grabbing his overalls strap and pulling him where he didn't want to go—behavior not uncommon to both the brothers when hungry or on a sugar high.

Linda was first to hear the dogs' bark and Faustine's Suburban slide to a halt in the gravel driveway. She looked out the window in time to see him jump out, carelessly dragging a rifle.

"Nina . . . *Cuidado! Aqui viene las problemas. Faustine está aqui y parece loco!*"

Before Nina could dry her hands on her apron Faustine was upon them, storming into the kitchen demanding to take the boys. "*Dame los hermanos con prisa.* They're going with me! Now! *No estoy bromeando, mujeres!*"

Nina told the boys to get under the table while Linda reached for the formidable looking stag-handled ice pick close by on the counter near the sink.

"Are you joking, Linda, an icepick against this deer rifle?" Faustine smirked.

Just then Rosendo came through the door from the dining room carrying his guitar and casually noodling a Beatles song on his guitar.

"Rosendo," Linda yelled. "He's crazy, get back! He's trying to take the boys! Yell to Lalo quick, he's with the sheep!"

Rosendo, backed out fast, ringing the meal bell on the porch and yelling to Lalo. Still in a kind of residual daze from his pot, he returned and walked straight up to Faustine, and before anyone else moved or even realized it, the youth swung his guitar hard at Faustine's head, breaking his beloved friend into two pieces, separating the body from the neck, leaving them hanging by the strings, and sending Faustine into a spiral, losing his balance, dropping his gun, and stumbling into Linda, knocking her to the floor.

Faustine screamed "*Bruja puta! Mujer fea!* What have you done, as he looked down to see the ice pick deep in his leg, sending squirts of blood and a jolt of excruciating pain throughout his body.

Nina, rushing to her children, yelled to her mom, "*Ojo de toro, mamacita!* You hit an artery, mom!

Faustine was cursing wildly, blabbering incoherently, and limping out the front door. The two little boys were crying and Rosendo was cradling what was left of his guitar, saying "*Que lastima! Lo siento ... Lo siento! Mi Paracho, Lo siento.*"

By the time Lalo came in to the kitchen, the preacher, leaving a trail of blood, had struggled into his Suburban and was speeding away in a haze of smoke and a jumble of noise, weaving back and forth on the road to the ruins.

Lalo, sizing up what had transpired, helped Linda

to her feet and into a chair, comforted Nina and his grandsons, and told Rosendo "Phone the sheriff, call Raul and tell him to meet me at the ruins!"

§

When Lalo entered the nearest ruin he passed by one or two tourists, and rushed to the docent asking her if she'd seen an enraged man, limping and bleeding from his leg; telling her also to call the sheriff in town.

The blood was visible enough to make tracking Faustine easy enough. Lalo found him in a corner, as life's ironies would have it, in the same place where he had proposed to Nina. He was now huddled in a crying ball and pressing both bloody hands on his injured leg.

Lalo raised his 257 Roberts at the whimpering miscreant, pointing it at his head and said, "You're done *pendejo*! Done!"

But he couldn't do it; couldn't pull the trigger, seeing only one of his sheep injured, and asking for mercy with its eyes.

Lalo then just hunkered down, reached for a

cigarette in his shirt pocket, lit up with a flip of his Zippo, and watched the wretch of a man against the mud wall in the corner of a ruin bleed out and die like a sheep sacrificed to God or Devil in atonement.

When Raul arrived he found Lalo and the preacher and he too hunkered down beside his brother, lit a cigarette and said nothing.

Only the sheriff's deputy when he got there had any words to say. "*Qué pasa, amigos? Qué pasa? Hay mucho sangre! Pobrecito! Qué lastima! Esta muerto!*"

EPILOGUE:
AL QUÉ QUIERRE

People don't always get what they want. Life is full of sadness and tragedy. The Spanish in particular know the tragic sense of life: *La tristeza de la vida, El sentido de la vida tragico*. The people, the characters, in this story, this fiction suffered yet always somehow found the resilience to carry on.

Let's imagine that Nina moved to Albuquerque with her two sons, married Anthony and together built a thriving fitness business, developing a series of videos and demonstrations which allowed them to build a new home, including their own private gym. Eloy and Eddie followed them in the business.

Rosendo became a professional guitarist and composer much revered for his solo guitar recordings and method books on smooth Latin jazz *"con clave."*

Lalo and Linda lived to an old age capped by sixty plus years of marriage. Lalo's sheep breeding and raising theories were adopted throughout the industry and greeted universally with gratitude as innovative.

They willed the ranch to Raul and Estelle and their daughters, with thirty acres bestowed to Nina and her new family. Those acres were developed as a shooting range and a field for self-defense and combat training for SWAT and K-9 police units.

Raul was tapped to administer those activities, continuing his sheep raising legacy, supplemented by guiding hunters into the mountains in search of deer, bear, and occasional elk. He vowed too that he had seen and would eventually prove the existence of a ghost jaguar.

The church, the congregation and a few other preachers came and went, eventually giving way to televangelism and mega churches in nearby big cities.

And the ruins? They still stand, casting a long architectural and historical shadow of enchantment across the inland ocean of the llano and the varied climatic and geological zones of the Southwest—a land continuing to shock and assuage the humanity living through the future and the next surprises of space travel in a timeless land where the ancient and the modern converge in new beliefs, new knowledge, new religions.

READERS GUIDE

1. Who is the ideal reader for this short novel? Offer a profile.

2. Setting plays a prominent role in the story. Identify key locales via a published map or one you draw.

3. Is this strictly a regional, Western, narrative without any universal application?

4. Could any aspects of plot or theme be considered universal?

5. Is the subtitle a cornerstone of the theme or merely a useful building brick among many?

6. Do you find the characters flat and static or do they round out and grow?

7. This is predominately Nina's story, agreed? But who equally attracts the reader's attention? In what way?

8. Many short novels have a closed ending. In what ways does this one invite a sequel?

9. The role of family is presented somewhat ambivalently here—at times positive and at times not. So what?

10. How important are animals to the story? Do they rise to the importance of characters?

11. Is this a satire? Is religion satirized or out and out disparaged?

12. Could this story be classified as magic realism? Why or why not?

13. Trace the blood imagery found throughout and how is it associated with guilt?

14. Is the pastor's descent into delusion and paranoia credible? Is religion the cause?

15. Does charismatic religion, and the Bible seeming to sanction it, to your liking?

16. Could Nina's guitarist brother be written out of the story? Why not?

17. Any classic, stereotypical villains here? Any character foils in general?

18. In what way is the ending foreshadowed?

19. Bloodguilt is a theme common to the Bible and to Renaissance tragedies of blood like *Macbeth* and *Hamlet*. Any modern applications?

20. What influences do the ruins have on tone and atmosphere?

21. Do the critical terms *Bildungsroman* and *Kunstler roman* have relevance to the story? How so?

22. Is a trigger warning needed about rape and shocking sexuality?

23. Give some thought to hunting and to the moral questions associated with slaughtering of animals. Any insights given to the issues here?

24. Is snake handling and worship, dramatized as ironic, comic, frightening, or boring?

25. Which disturbs you the most—reading about human death or animal death?

www.ingramcontent.com/pod-product-compliance
Lightning Source LLC
Chambersburg PA
CBHW011936050726
47590CB00011B/3320